JEWEL OF CANAAN

The Brave Beauty Series
Volume 1

Jewel of Canaan

A Story Adapted from the Book of Judges

MARION DAWSON GUNDERSON

Interior Drawings by Susan Shorter

WESTBOW
PRESS
A DIVISION OF THOMAS NELSON

Illustrations by Susan Shorter

Scripture taken from the Holy Bible, New International Version®. Copyright © 1973, 1978, 1984 Biblica. Used by permission of Zondervan. All rights reserved.

WestBow Press books may be ordered through booksellers or by contacting:

WestBow Press
A Division of Thomas Nelson
1663 Liberty Drive
Bloomington, IN 47403
www.westbowpress.com
1-(866) 928-1240

ISBN: 978-1-4497-5202-6 (sc)
ISBN: 978-1-4497-5203-3 (e)

Library of Congress Control Number: 2012908396

Printed in the United States of America

WestBow Press rev. date: 09/20/2012

CONTENTS

For Kira

1

SPRING

Long ago in the land of Canaan, there lived a little girl named Deborah, a name that means *bee*. Deborah loved to play among the wildflowers that covered the hills near her village. She tagged along with her older brothers, Zev and Carmie, when they explored Canaan's rocky cliffs and dark caves.

Deborah grew into a beautiful young woman. Her skin was a radiant bronze from days spent in the sun. Shiny black hair framed her lovely face. Young men went out of their way to catch a glimpse of her when she worked at the weaving loom in the courtyard, or when she watched her twin sisters, Ariel and Alissa.

One morning, when Deborah and her mother were outside for a few minutes, Ariel and Alissa decided to make butter. They'd seen Deborah do it many times, and it looked like fun. Ariel took down the bag of milk from its peg in the kitchen, grabbed its leather strings, and began swinging it around like a windmill blade. After a few swings, Alissa shouted, "That's not how to do it! Let *me!*"

"No, it's still my turn," said Ariel.

"Let go! It's mine!" demanded Alissa. She reached for the strings.

"No, *you* let go! I had it first," cried Ariel. The twins pulled furiously, stretching the strings between them. Alissa gave it her hardest tug, yanking the strings out of Ariel's hands. The bag thudded to the floor, splashing the precious milk everywhere.

"*Now* see what you've done!" cried Ariel, wiping milk off her feet. "Wait until Mama sees this."

Just then, Deborah appeared in the doorway, carrying a jug of water. Seeing the spill, she exclaimed, "What in the world—"

"It's Alissa's fault!" cried Ariel. "I had it first, and she—"

"It was *my* turn!" shouted Alissa.

"We'll settle this later," said Deborah, setting the heavy jug on the floor. "For now, you two need to clean up this mess." She handed each girl a rag.

"But I—" objected Alissa.

"No more arguing!" said Deborah. "After you've mopped up the milk, take some of this water and rinse it down. We don't want this house smelling sour when Mama gets back."

The twins sank to their knees, and began mopping silently. Deborah watched them with a stern expression that masked the deep affection she felt for her little sisters. "Let me know when you're done," she said quietly. "There's one more thing we need to do."

"Deborah, Alissa, Ariel! I'm home!" called Mama.

We're out here, Mama!" called Deborah. Mama entered the kitchen, pausing to set some bundles of yarn on the table. She pushed open the door to the milking shed. Her three daughters were crouched around a nervous she-goat.

"We're having a milking lesson," said Deborah. Ariel pulled and squeezed as the milk squirted into a clay jar.

"I got the most milk!" bragged Alissa.

"Did not," countered Ariel. "I'm not done yet."

"Stop boasting," said Deborah. "You've both done very well. I'm proud of you."

"I'm proud of *all* my girls!" beamed Mama.

"Alright girls," said Deborah, "We've milked this goat dry." She walked to a nearby wall and, using a small etching stone, scratched the days of the week into the chalky surface while Mama and the twins watched.

"Since you're both good at milking," began Deborah, "you'll each have a milking day. Tomorrow will be Ariel's day; the next day will be Alissa's. Deborah wrote their names under their milking days.

"What about making butter?" asked Ariel.

"Today will be Alissa's day to make butter."

"But the milk got spilled!" blurted Alissa. She quickly cupped her hand over her mouth and looked at Mama.

"Oh?" said Mama.

"I'll tell you about it later, Mama," said Deborah. She turned to the twins. "Alissa will make the butter tomorrow. For now, you two go play in the courtyard. If you behave yourselves, I'll teach you how to make flower crowns."

"Yay!" chorused the twins as they scrambled out of the shed.

Deborah followed Mama back to the kitchen. "They were fighting over the milk bag and spilled the whole thing," she said. "I made them clean it up."

"They did a fine job," said Mama. "I didn't notice a thing."

"I thought it was time they learned how much work it takes to get a bag of milk."

"You were their age when you learned to milk. I can't believe you're already old enough to marry."

"But Mama! I want to stay here and help you and Papa! You need my help, don't you?"

"I know you'll always help us, sweet one, but we must think about your future. Papa loves you and will find a good husband for you. For now, we need to think about Zev's wedding." Deborah's oldest brother, Zev, was engaged to a lovely girl named Miriam. They planned to be married in the fall. Mama showed Deborah the bundles of yarn and said, "I'm going to weave these into a sleeping mat for them."

"The colors are perfect!" exclaimed Deborah. "I know they'll love it Mama." She started toward the back door. "I think I'll see how the garden is doing."

As she stepped into the spring sunlight, Deborah thought, *I wish I could choose my own husband!*

2

A PROMISE

Ariel held up a chain of wild marigolds. "Is this good?"

"*Very* good, Ariel!" said Deborah. "It's almost long enough."

"Mine's longer!' boasted Alissa.

"This isn't a contest," said Deborah. "It's better to do a good job than be the first one done." The three sisters sat in a sunny field of wildflowers. Honeysuckle crept over the rocks, its sweet scent wafting through the late afternoon air. Birds twittered nearby as they gathered last year's grasses for their nests.

"How long before we leave for Passover?" asked Ariel.

"Just three more days," said Deborah.

"I get to ride the donkey first!" cried Alissa.

"Since you just put yourself ahead of your sister," said Deborah, "you will be *last* to ride the donkey. You should put others first." Alissa frowned and resumed weaving her flower chain.

"Deborah, why do we have Passover?" asked Ariel. "I hate it when the priest kills the lambs."

"We do it to remind us that God freed our people from slavery in Egypt. That was over two hundred years ago. Passover helps us remember."

"I like the part about the *plagues*," said Ariel. "Especially the frog plague, and the grasshopper plague, and—"

"And the plague of blood!" cried Alissa.

"The important thing is *why* God sent those terrible plagues," said Deborah. "The pharaoh wanted to keep our people in Egypt to do all the work. It took *ten plagues* before he finally let them go!"

"I wish we could just remember it without killing the lambs," said Ariel.

"I know," said Deborah. "I hate that part too. But it helps us remember the tenth plague; the one with a promise."

"What was the tenth plague?" asked Ariel. "I forgot."

"It was the plague of the death angel," said Deborah. "Our people put lambs' blood over their doors so the death angel would 'pass over' their houses and not kill anyone inside."

Alissa looked up from her work. "You said it was the plague with a promise."

"Yes. God promised to send his *own* Lamb for everybody. After that, we won't have to kill *our* lambs anymore. God's Lamb will pay for all the bad things we do."

"I just hope he sends his Lamb before Passover!" said Ariel.

Deborah tied the ends of the flower chains to form two rings, then placed them on the girls' heads. "There," she said. "Two princesses!"

The three sisters sprang to their feet, and pranced about the meadow, stopping to gather flowers for Mama. Suddenly, they heard angry shouts in the distance. They stopped and peered in the direction of the sheep pen. Only Deborah could see over the tall grass. Two men strode toward the village. "It's Zev and Carmie," said Deborah. "Zev's carrying something."

The girls hurried down the hill toward home. When they arrived, only Mama was inside. Papa was outside by the garden talking to Zev and Carmie. He sounded angry. Carmie kept saying, "I'm sorry, Papa."

Mama was kneading bread dough, her lips pinched tightly together. "What happened, Mama?" asked Deborah.

"Carmie made a mistake," said Mama without looking up.

"What kind of mistake?"

"Never mind." Mama glanced at her daughters. "Papa will decide what to do. Now, I need the three of you to help with supper. Deborah, please shape this dough and set it in by oven."

"Yes, Mama."

"Alissa and Ariel, please wash your hands and set the table." The twins hurried to the washbasin.

"And girls," said Mama with a smile, "Your flower crowns are lovely."

After a while, Zev and Carmie left the yard and headed back to the sheep pasture. Deborah noticed Zev carrying a lamb. Papa entered the house wearing a troubled look, and sank into his favorite chair without a word. Mama and the girls quietly busied themselves.

When supper was ready, Mama placed two bowls of lentil stew and a loaf of warm bread in a basket, then added a pouch of wine. "Deborah," she said, "please take this to your brothers."

"Yes, Mama," said Deborah. She stepped outside, strode past the garden, and climbed the hill toward the pasture thinking, *What could Carmie have done to make Papa so angry?*

When Deborah arrived at the sheep pen, Zev and Carmie were herding the last of the flock in for the night. Zev was the oldest. He was known in the village for his skill in protecting the sheep. He'd never lost a single one to the lions, hyenas, and bears that roamed Canaan in those days.

Carmie hadn't taken to shepherding as well. He had a soft heart for the animals. When one of them died, he grieved for days.

"Your supper has arrived!" announced Deborah with forced cheeriness.

"Just put it there," said Zev flatly, pointing to a wooden stool near the pen.

Deborah set down the basket and approached Zev, who was locking the gate.

"I noticed you were carrying a lamb," she said.

"Yes, I was," said Zev.

"I hope it wasn't injured," offered Deborah.

"No, it wasn't injured—exactly."

"Oh? What happened to it—exactly?"

"It was *spoiled!*" Zev shot a searing glance at Carmie, who had settled onto a tree stump with his supper. Carmie stopped chewing and stared at his food.

"Spoiled?" prodded Deborah.

"Alright, I'll tell you so you won't keep asking about it. Carmie made a pet of our best lamb. He named it and talked to it like it was a baby. He didn't want it killed for Passover, so he stained it with some dye he made from henna leaves."

Deborah scanned the flock. She spotted a white lamb with red dye splashed across its fleece. Carmie looked up at Deborah, his face flushed with shame. "I'm sorry," he said.

"I'm sorry too, Carmie," said Deborah "What did Papa say?"

"He hasn't decided my punishment yet."

Zev and Carmie ate their supper in silence. Deborah sat near Carmie, patting him reassuringly.

Finally, Deborah gathered up the dishes and placed them in the basket. "Have a good night. See you in the morning." She started toward the village, then turned back and called, "I love you both the same!"

3

PASSOVER

The family started their Passover trip to Shiloh on a warm spring morning when the fields were dotted with purple iris. Deborah led the donkey, with Ariel happily perched on the animal for the first part of the trip. Alissa skipped alongside asking, "Is it my turn yet?" until Deborah warned her to stop asking or she wouldn't get a turn at all.

Mama and Papa followed on foot. Carmie came last, glumly pulling a lamb in a wagon. The animal bleated unhappily. Zev had stayed home to tend the flock.

The road was crowded with other Israelite families from the hill country, all going to worship at Shiloh. In those days, the Israelite temple was a large tent called a *tabernacle*.

Mama turned to Papa. "Couldn't *you* present the lamb to the priest the way you always do?"

"Carmie needs to do it this time," said Papa. "He ruined our best lamb."

"I understand," said Mama, "but it's a painful lesson."

"It is. At first, I didn't know how to punish him. He gets so attached to the lambs. Finally, I asked Deborah. She has great wisdom for her age."

"Yes," said Mama. "She's wise beyond her years. People ask her for advice all the time."

"She said I should make Carmie correct his own mistake, so I made him choose another lamb."

"That makes sense," said Mama. After a thoughtful pause, she said, "What *about* Carmie? His talent certainly isn't shepherding!"

"I know," said Papa. "When we get back, I'll put him in charge of the vineyard."

"Wonderful! He loves tending the grapes. But who'll help Zev with the sheep?"

"*I* will!" said Papa. "I want to spend more time with him before he marries."

Suddenly Ariel pointed to the road ahead and shouted, "Look, Deborah! What's that?"

Deborah boosted herself onto the donkey behind Ariel, and scanned the road. A cloud of dust rose in the distance. Horsemen emerged from it, followed by chariots. Foot travelers scattered to the sides of the road.

"It's the army!" shouted Deborah. "Make way for the army!" Her warning spread through the crowd. Soon mounted horsemen could be seen, their helmets glinting in the sun.

"Sisera's troops!" shouted Papa. "No doubt they've come to raid our homes while we're gone! It isn't enough that they take our crops!" The Israelites had no king of their own, but were ruled by a cruel Canaanite king

named Jabin. He had no interest in the Israelites except for what he could steal from them. His general, Sisera, had made the king rich by raiding villages.

As the troops drew closer, donkeys and sheep panicked. Carmie scooped up the lamb to comfort it. The twins clung to Mama and Papa. Deborah pulled the frightened donkey to safety.

General Sisera led the march, sitting pompously astride a huge battle stallion that strained under the general's armor-clad body. White foam dripped from the animal's mouth. Sisera sneered down at the Israelites with obvious contempt. He was followed by dozens of mounted warriors armed with spears and battle-axes.

As the chariots rumbled closer, a second wave of panic swept through the livestock. Deborah pulled the donkey further away from the road. She stood next to Papa, watching the marauders thunder past. Each chariot bore two drivers whipping their horses relentlessy.

"Don't worry Papa," said Deborah. We've hidden everything." She and Mama had stored the food and tools in the caves Deborah knew about.

"And Zev took the sheep to the high pasture," said Papa. "That's one place these chariots can't go."

As the convoy disappeared toward the village, Deborah silently prayed, *Please, Lord, protect our homes!*

4

SUMMER

Summer came early in Canaan. By June, the grain was ripe, and the whole village helped with the harvest. Men cut the stalks with rhythmic swings of their sickles. Women and children followed behind, tying the stalks into sheaves. They sang and talked as they worked. It was a happy time for the villagers.

During the harvest, young men looked for maidens who might be ready for marriage. One such man was Lappidoth, a name that means *lightning flashes*. Everyone called him Lapp. He was the same age as Deborah's brother, Zev. Lapp and Zev often hunted together. Whenever they returned from a hunt, Lapp brought bouquets of wildflowers to Deborah and Mama.

The villagers admired Lapp's carpentry skills and his generosity. When Mama's weaving loom was smashed by Sisera's troops in the Passover raid, Lapp quickly built her a new one.

When the harvesters gathered under the ancient oak trees for lunch, Deborah found herself scanning the clusters of young men for a glimpse of Lapp. When she spotted him, he was often returning her gaze.

One day, near the end of the harvest, the twins burst into the house at suppertime. "Mama!" shouted Alissa. "Mr. Lapp is coming to visit!"

"He gave Deborah flowers!" exclaimed Ariel. Deborah stepped through the doorway clutching a bouquet of lilies.

"This *is* exciting news!" said Mama. She sent the twins to wash their hands, then turned to Deborah. "Well daughter, what's this all about?"

"Papa asked Lapp to build Zev's new house. They're meeting here tonight."

"Hmm. It sounds like Papa has more in mind than planning a house."

"I know what you mean, Mama. He wants to know if Lapp would be a good husband for me."

"How do *you* feel about it, sweet one?"

Deborah blushed. She began arranging the lilies in a clay jar while trying to sort out her feelings.

"Well?' persisted Mama.

"I've always liked Lapp, Mama."

"He's a fine man, Deborah."

"I know. He's very kind."

"He certainly is," agreed Mama.

"And he's fun to talk to."

"Yes. He always has something good to say about people."

"But none of those things is most important to me, Mama."

"Oh? What *is* most important?"

"I just want to have the *right* husband, the one God wants for me."

"I'm sure Papa wants that for you, too."

That summer was an exciting time for Deborah. Lapp often appeared at the door in the evening wearing a clean tunic and holding a bouquet of flowers. He would sit on the flat roof of the house with Papa and Carmie talking about crops, hunting, and Zev's new house. They could see Deborah's garden below. It was bursting with onions, garlic, beans, cucumbers, and melons, enough to share with the whole village.

Deborah wore her prettiest gown for Lapp's visits. She hovered around the men, serving fresh figs, raisin cakes, and melon. Lapp was so distracted by Deborah's beauty—and the scent of her homemade rose perfume—that he could barely follow the conversation.

One evening, Papa was telling how Sisera was getting bolder and raiding villages even when people were home. There were reports of villagers taken as slaves.

"We have no weapons," said Lapp.

"Just axes and hunting bows," said Carmie.

Suddenly, Deborah broke into the conversation. "We should dig secret cellars to store our food," she said. "We may have to live in the hills." The men were startled by the authority in Deborah's voice. She said nothing else, but continued serving snacks as if she'd said nothing at all.

5

FALL

"Alright you two, you've had enough," shouted Carmie. "If you eat any more, you'll have bellyaches!" Carmie stood in the stone tower watching the twins gorge themselves on the first grapes of the season. "Now take that basket and pick some for Mama!" The girls began dropping the purple fruit into a basket.

"Carmie, how long until we get to stomp the grapes?" called Alissa.

"About two weeks!" said Carmie. The crop was ripening fast. *It will be a big harvest,* thought Carmie. *God is good to us, even though I spoiled his Passover lamb.*

From the stone watchtower in the vineyard, Carmie could see the whole countryside; the top of Mount Tabor to the distant north; a flock of white storks overhead winging their way to Africa for the winter; the olive grove to the west; the pasture dotted with fat sheep. He surveyed the village below with its flat roofs hung with strings of dates and figs drying in the autumn sun.

He could see Deborah kneeling on the rocky hillside near the village, digging crocus bulbs. She would use them for a special wedding gift she was making for

Zev and Miriam. *Only six more weeks until the wedding*, she thought. She was excited about being a bridesmaid, and happy to be gaining Miriam as a new sister.

When she returned to the village, Deborah found Mama and the twins in the courtyard heating a kettle of grapes and honey. After the mixture thickened, it would be served warm with bread and butter.

"Let me stir first!" cried Alissa.

"What did I hear?" asked Deborah.

"Uh, I'll stir after you, Ariel," said Alissa.

"That's better."

"Hello, ladies!" It was Lapp's familiar voice. He was leaving for the day after working on Zev's house.

"Lapp!" said Mama, "I understand you've started on the roof."

"Yes, ma'am, we have. It should be done in plenty of time for the wedding—and before the early rains." Lapp smiled at Deborah, trying not to linger too long on her beautiful face.

Deborah felt embarrassed standing there in her digging clothes. She hoped Lapp wouldn't notice her grimy gown and dirty fingernails.

"We appreciate all your help, Lapp," said Mama.

"I'm happy to do it, ma'am," said Lapp. "It's good practice for building my *own* house someday." He smiled at Deborah. She felt her face flush and her heart beat faster.

"Mama, are these gowns alright for grape stomping?" asked Ariel. The twins were dressed in old ragged gowns.

"I see they're still long enough to cover your knees. Yes, those will do," said Mama.

The twins were now old enough to stomp grapes in the village winepress. Deborah would go with them in case they got frightened or fell down in the slippery vat. Later that morning, Mama, Papa, and the three girls crossed the courtyard and climbed the low hill where a crowd of villagers was already gathered. Carmie and the other growers were dumping baskets of grapes into the winepress. It was already two feet deep in the fragrant fruit.

Deborah and the twins joined the excited villagers who were washing their feet in a cold spring. "Ooo!" exclaimed Ariel, jerking her toes from the icy water.

"If you want to stomp, you have to wash your feet," said Deborah. The twins drew in their breath and eased into the water. "That's my brave girls," encouraged Deborah, kneeling to scrub the four little feet.

When the foot washing was done, Deborah led the shivering girls up the path of woven mats that led to the winepress. They arrived in time to hear the foreman shout, "Let the winemaking begin!"

Dozens of villagers leaped into the winepress, and began gleefully crushing the fruit with their feet. Deborah climbed in, then lowered each twin into the vat. "Eee!" squealed Ariel. "It feels so squishy!"

"Let go!" cried Alissa, wrenching her hand from Deborah and charging ahead. Soon the onlookers broke into a chant, and clapped to the rhythm. The stompers took up the beat, transforming the work into a joyful dance. Mama and Papa clapped and sang as they watched their three daughters join in the fun.

Lapp was working in a crew of men who were draining the juice into crocks where it would ferment into wine. Every so often, he glanced at Deborah.

The stomping went on all day. As workers tired, others took their places. Miriam didn't join the stomping; she was too busy getting ready for her wedding.

6

THE WEDDING DAY

In ancient Israel, only the groom knew exactly when the wedding would be. It would take place about a year after he had visited the maiden with gifts for her father and spoken a promise to her; *I am going to prepare a place for you. When it is ready, I will come again and take you home with me.*

It had been a year since Zev had made the promise to Miriam, so he could come for her at any time. She had her clothes and kitchen supplies in baskets. Her bridal gown hung near her bed.

The bridegroom would typically come for his bride in the evening, when the villagers could be there to see the ceremony and join in the celebration. The bridesmaids kept their lamps filled with oil so they could rush to the bride and escort her to her wedding, and her new home.

At his chosen time, the bridegroom would don a crown of olive branches, collect his groomsmen, and sound a ram's horn called a *shofar* to proclaim that he was coming for his bride.

"There," said Deborah, as she hung a wreath in Zev and Miriam's new home. The wreath was an artful arrangement of dried flowers, ribbons, and crocus bulbs.

"It's perfect," said Mama. "I hope they'll be happy here."

"I wonder when Zev will blow the shofar."

"Not even the groomsmen know," said Mama, "but *we're* ready!"

Evening passed without the sound of the shofar. Deborah made sure her oil lamp was full. Her bridesmaid outfit hung on the wall. It was a pale green gown and scarf she had trimmed with a flower pattern stitched in colored threads.

The next day, Zev climbed to a grove where the last of the olives hung ripening. He cut some small branches, and sat quietly weaving himself a groom's crown.

That afternoon, when Deborah was in the courtyard grinding grain, a shofar sounded. She hurried home, shaking flour from her apron. Inside, Mama was helping the excited twins into their flower girl dresses. "Alissa, hold still!" pleaded Mama.

"Mama, Zev must be anxious to get married," said Deborah. "It's still *afternoon!*"

"He's always been my impatient one," said Mama, as she wrestled Alissa into her dress.

Deborah poured fresh water into a bowl, and rinsed the flour from her skin. The shofar sounded again. Deborah thought happily about the day the shofar would sound for her. She slipped into her bridesmaid gown, donned her headscarf, and picked up her oil lamp. "I'm off to attend the bride!" she chimed, emerging from her room.

"Look at Deborah!" cried Ariel. "She looks so *beau*-tee-ful!"

The shofar sounded again. "Zev should stop blowing that horn and get down here!" declared Mama.

"It sounds like he's invented a new wedding call," said Deborah. It sounded unfamiliar. "See you soon!"

She headed for Miriam's house. When she arrived, Miriam was radiant in her bridal gown. Bridesmaids were arranging her veil.

"Miriam! You look lovely!" exclaimed Deborah. "I hope Zev doesn't faint from excitement when he sees you!" The women laughed at the thought. Some of them slid Miriam's baskets toward the door, where Zev's groomsmen would collect them.

Suddenly, shouting came from the courtyard; "It's the alarm! The alarm is sounding!" Men raced in from the fields. The shofar sounded again. It *wasn't* the wedding call!

"So *that's* why it kept sounding!" cried Deborah.

Miriam's father appeared in the doorway, his face white with fear. "Miriam!" he cried, "I'm so sorry, daughter, but Sisera's troops are attacking us! Hurry to safety!"

Miriam stood frozen, unable to grasp what was happening. Deborah grabbed her by the shoulders. "You *will* marry Zev!" she said. "Now go and hide!" Relatives pulled Miriam toward the back door and the safety of the hills, while Deborah dashed out the front, and ran for home.

The courtyard was a confusion of frantic women, bawling children, and panicked animals. Village men charged about with axes and garden tools. Sisera's soldiers emerged from houses lugging sacks of grain and jugs of oil. They piled the stolen goods into wagons while fending off villagers with clubs and spears.

Mama emerged from the dust with the twins in tow. Grabbing Alissa's hand, Deborah shouted, "Mama! Bring Ariel and follow me!" She headed for the safety of the hills. The ground shook as chariots rumbled into the courtyard.

"Deborah!" screamed Mama. Deborah spun around to see Mama clutching Ariel as a soldier tried to pry the screaming girl away from her. A second soldier leaped from a chariot and struck Mama with his beefy forearm, knocking her to the ground.

Soldiers grabbed Ariel and threw her into the chariot where rough hands quickly bound her in rope. The driver cracked his whip, setting the vehicle in motion. Ariel screamed, "Mama! Don't let them take me!"

Carmie appeared out of the mayhem, racing toward home. "Carmie!" shouted Deborah, pointing to the chariot, "They have Ariel!" Carmie charged after the chariot, jumped aboard and tried to wrestle the frantic child from her captors.

"Carmie!" wailed Ariel. "Help me!" One of the drivers struck Carmie with an iron bar, knocking him over the side of the chariot. His foot became lodged in the spokes of the churning wheel. Its rotation slammed him to the ground, leaving his leg limp and mangled.

Deborah, Mama, and Alissa watched in horror as the chariot disappeared in a cloud of dust, leaving Carmie broken on the ground. He tried to struggle to his feet, but his leg crumpled under him. As Deborah ran to him, Alissa yanked herself free and started running to where the chariot had vanished. "Ariel!" she shouted. "Ariel, I'm coming!"

Deborah grabbed Alissa and pulled her back. "Stop! They'll take you too!"

"But they *can't* take her!" wailed Alissa.

"Stay with *us!*" ordered Deborah, tightening her hold on Alissa and turning to Carmie, who now lay moaning on the ground. His skin was turning a grayish color. Only white showed beneath his fluttering eyelids.

Mama struggled to her feet, and hobbled to Carmie. "Oh God," she screamed. "Save him!"

"We must get him to safety, Mama!" cried Deborah. She began dragging Carmie from the courtyard, which was now a noisy din of distraught villagers and shouting soldiers. Mama and Alissa helped drag Carmie behind a house. Deborah knelt over her stricken brother. "We're safe now Carmie," she said. "You'll be fine. We're here, we're safe." *Please God, let him live!* she prayed.

Carmie's lips moved. "Ariel . . . Ariel," came his raspy voice. His body shuddered, and he sank into a deep sleep.

After what seemed like hours, the clamor died down. Deborah ventured into the courtyard in hopes of finding a blanket to stop Carmie's shivering. A few dazed men wandered about as the dust settled on the bodies of the dead and wounded.

"Deborah!" It was Papa, staggering toward her, his face bloody and swollen.

"Papa!" Deborah rushed to him, grateful to see him alive.

"Where's Mama?" asked Papa. "And why aren't you hiding with the others?"

"Carmie's injured, Papa. We stayed with him."

"Where?"

"Behind the widow's house. I must find a blanket for him." She started for home, then turned back. "Papa, what about Zev?"

"He's rounding up the sheep."

"And Lapp? Have you seen him?"

"I saw him felling a soldier with his axe! Are the twins safe?" Deborah drew in her breath, knowing she was about to deliver a dreadful blow.

"*Alissa* is safe, Papa," she said, her eyes filling with tears.

"And Ariel?" Papa frantically searched Deborah's face, trying to read its meaning. Deborah took Papa's hands.

"Papa, Ariel was…taken," said Deborah, her eyes brimming with tears.

"No!" roared Papa. "Not my little lamb!" he wailed. "Not my Ariel!" His face twisted in anguish. The two fell to their knees, clinging to each other as they dissolved into grief for the lost girl. Their dusty tears trickled down and mingled together on Deborah's bridesmaid dress.

7

WINTER

As the last dead leaves drifted down from Canaan's trees, life in the village ended. The people no longer felt safe in their homes, so they moved to the hills where they could hide from Sisera's troops. The roads became deserted, except for army patrols and traders taking supplies to King Jabin's castle in Hazor.

The villagers moved into caves for the winter. They had saved what was left of the village—garden vegetables that hadn't been trampled, some tools and furniture, and food they had wisely hidden in cellars. Zev had chased down the family donkey. Carmie survived his injuries, but could no longer stand or walk on his own. Lapp fashioned a crutch for him out of olivewood.

One evening, Deborah's family was gathered in their cave for supper. They sat on stools in a circle because they had no table. A single oil lamp illuminated their faces. When the meal was over, Carmie pulled himself up using his crutch, and stood on his one good leg. "I'm going to the vineyard," he announced.

"But Carmie," said Papa. "The vineyard was burned by the soldiers."

"Yes, Papa, but the vines will grow back from the roots. I'll dig some tonight, and start a vineyard here."

"What if you fall?" said Deborah. "Let me go with you."

"You just saw me get up!" objected Carmie.

"I'm sorry, Carmie," said Deborah. "I forgot how well you're doing."

"That's alright. I know you meant well." Carmie stooped and peered out at the darkening sky. "It's a full moon," he said. "I'll be back in a few hours." He slung a sack over his shoulder, and hobbled out into the night.

"He needs to do this," said Papa quietly. "God made him a vinedresser."

"Yes," agreed Mama. "And we can look forward to fresh grapes again!"

"Speaking of crops," said Deborah, "We must plant the winter grain. The early rains will come soon."

"But daughter, we have no seed!" exclaimed Papa.

"Yes, we do! I hid some."

"I should have known," smiled Papa. "You always think ahead. Lapp would do well to marry such a wise woman!" Papa was clearly in favor of Deborah and Lapp marrying. Deborah was anxious for the day when Lapp would come with gifts for Papa, an Israelite tradition that amounted to a promise of marriage.

"Deborah," said Papa, "We can't grow grain in these hills. The soil's too thin—and the soldiers took our plow."

"We don't have to plant it here, Papa. We can just scatter it in the old grain field by the village. We can work by moonlight!"

"But the soldiers will take it!"

"They're too lazy to harvest it, Papa. They only steal grain in sacks!" They laughed at the thought of the pompous troops doing fieldwork.

As usual, Alissa sat glumly at the table, as she had since Ariel was taken. She couldn't shake the memory of her twin disappearing in the chariot. Her mind was tormented with questions. *Where is she? Are they cruel to her? Does she cry for us the way we cry for her? Does she have a new mother? A new sister?*

Alissa wondered whether Ariel was alive or dead, but she never spoke of it. Thoughts of it came to her in nightmares that left her screaming in the dark cave. Deborah slept with her so she could soothe her little sister back to sleep.

Zev and Miriam lived in a nearby cave. They had married in a quiet ceremony. There had been no shofar sounding, and no bridal parade. Miriam had escaped from the village with only her wedding gown.

8

A PROPOSAL

One sunny afternoon in early spring, Deborah sat outside the family cave weaving on a new loom Lapp had built. Hearing footsteps, she looked up to see Lapp walking toward her carrying a bundle of poles.

"Good Morning, Deborah!" he called.

"Good Morning, Lapp! Where are you off to?"

"Zev and Miriam's cave. They're building a storage hut." Lapp stopped in front of Deborah. "Actually, I was hoping to see you." He smiled warmly.

"Oh?" Deborah felt hope rising in her spirit.

Lapp propped the poles against a tree, walked back to Deborah, and said, "Deborah, can we talk?"

"Certainly! Let me tell Mama." Deborah rushed to the cave entrance, her heart leaping with excitement. She poked her head inside, and told Mama that she and Lapp would be talking under the acacia tree. Mama smiled knowingly, and waved her out.

This is it! thought Deborah. *He's going to ask me!*

Deborah led Lapp on a carpet of blue hyacinths to the shade of the acacia tree. They sat on the wooden bench Zev had rescued from the village. They gazed out at a field of wild tulips just beginning to show color.

Lapp turned to Deborah, cleared his throat nervously, and looked steadily into her eyes. He spoke the words he had carefully rehearsed. "Deborah, your father has consented to let me bring gifts to him, as a promise of marriage—but only if it pleases you."

"Yes, it does please me—very much!" exclaimed Deborah. She felt dizzy with happiness. She gripped the bench to steady herself.

Lapp sighed in relief. "May I call on you tomorrow evening?"

"Of course!" They exchanged long, happy smiles. They were aching to hug each other, but that would have to wait.

"Deborah, there's something I want you to know," said Lapp in a more serious tone.

"Oh?" *Is Lapp about to reveal some dark secret?*

"Well, you're very special to me." Deborah suddenly felt self-conscious. She stared into her lap.

"I know," she said in a quiet voice.

"Deborah, I'm not your *only* admirer."

"Oh?" Deborah looked up, startled that Lapp might have a rival for her affection.

"The *whole village* admires you, Deborah. You told us to dig the secret cellars. You led us to the caves and the good water. You had all that food stored away. You found the roots and berries for us. If it weren't for you, we'd be starving right now."

"But it was just common sense!" objected Deborah.

"There is nothing *common* about your sense, Deborah! That's my point. Everyone admires your power to see ahead. Most people can barely see the next step in front of them. You seem to know what will happen in the future. Some people are even saying you're—" Lapp hesitated to use the word. "They say you're a *prophet.*"

"A *prophet?*" exclaimed Deborah. "How can I be a prophet? Prophets are *men!*"

"I know," said Lapp. "If not a prophet, then a judge. Israel hasn't had a judge for a long time."

"But judges are men, too," said Deborah.

"There's nothing in the sacred books that says women can't be leaders," said Lapp. "But listen, my love. There are more reasons. When the shepherds were squabbling over pastures, you stepped in and brought peace. When families were fighting over food, you showed them how to share it so that everyone would have enough. Now we're all working together. You have *wisdom;* everyone knows that."

"That may be true, but—"

"There's one more thing," said Lapp, "God's Word is written in your mind—and your heart. You know the holy writings as well as any priest at the tabernacle."

"Papa taught me," said Deborah. She was uneasy that the conversation had taken such a serious turn. "Lapp, what does all this have to do with our *engagement?*"

Lapp reached for Deborah's hand. "Deborah," he said, "I just want you to know that, when I'm your husband, I'll support you in whatever God calls you to do. I'll be your *protector.*"

Deborah realized the depth of Lapp's love. She knew most men would be too prideful to let their wives lead. Her eyes began to tear up. "I may be wise, Lapp, but you are the *rarest* of men!"

"I don't know about that," said Lapp, "but I *do* know it's time for me to deliver those poles. May I call on you tomorrow at sunset?"

"We'll be waiting!"

Deborah watched Lapp gather the poles and make his way down the hill. She looked at the hand he'd just held. She whispered, "What a blessed woman I am!"

The next day at sunset, Deborah and Papa seated themselves at the family table. Deborah was radiant in a white homespun gown. A ring of dainty white blossoms nestled in her hair.

Three lamps lit the cave for the ceremony, a lavish use of scarce olive oil. Mama placed an empty wooden goblet in front of Deborah, and then sat down on a bench near the wall. Alissa settled into Mama's lap. Carmie leaned on his crutch. They waited.

As the minutes ticked by, Alissa asked endless questions. "When will they get married? Am I old enough to be a bridesmaid? Will Deborah still sleep next to me, in case I have a nightmare? Will I have to do all the milking?"

"Shh!" said Mama. "I hear something!" It was the clomping of donkey hooves. Papa stepped outside.

"Peace to you, sir!" said Lapp.

"And peace to you!" answered Papa.

"I wish to present a covenant of gifts to you, that I might have the hand of your eldest daughter in marriage."

"You have my blessing!" answered Papa. "Please come in."

Lapp lifted two bulging sacks from the donkey, and tethered a small she-goat to a nearby sapling. The animal bleated briefly, then curled up and went to sleep.

Lapp followed Papa into the cave, and set the sacks on the floor. When he saw Deborah smiling at him in the lamplight, he was astonished anew at her beauty. He could barely take his eyes off her as he nodded greetings to the rest of the family, who now became silent witnesses to the ceremony.

Papa took his place next to Deborah. Lapp opened the largest sack and pulled out a jar of precious olive oil. Papa accepted it with gratitude. Next came a new wooden mallet and a shepherd's crook. The last gifts for Papa were a sturdy wooden plow for tilling a garden and a little sack of coins, the last of Lapp's money.

"Thank you, my son," said a teary-eyed Papa. He was overwhelmed by Lapp's generosity.

Everyone stared at the second sack. Though it wasn't required, a marriage covenant sometimes included gifts for the maiden. "And now for my lovely bride-to-be," said Lapp. Alissa craned her neck to see the new treasures. The first gift for Deborah was a new leather bag for making butter. Alissa stared at it, recalling the day she and Ariel had fought over the milk bag. She regretted the times she'd been selfish toward her twin.

Next came a new spinning wheel and a sack of wool. Deborah felt a surge of joy at the thought of making clothes for her family. Then Lapp presented Deborah with a clay water jug, some hand-carved bowls, and a milking jar. *When did he find time to make all this?* she thought. *The Lord has blessed me with a wonderful provider!*

"Now," said Lapp, "something to go with the milking jar." He stepped outside and returned with the sleepy goat. Everyone laughed as Lapp set the gangly animal down next to Deborah.

Alissa ran to the goat, and began stroking its woolly head. "She's so cute!, Deborah! May I name her?"

"Of course!" said Deborah.

"Alissa!" scolded Mama. "Let Mr. Lapp finish!" Alissa scooped up the goat, kissed it on the head, and returned to Mama's lap.

"There's one more gift," said Lapp. He reached for a small drawstring pouch that hung from his belt. He handed it to Deborah. Smiling shyly, she drew it open, and pulled out a shiny silver bracelet set with jewels, each one a different color.

"Oh, Lapp!" exclaimed Deborah. "It's beautiful!" As she admired the bracelet, she realized that the jewels were tiny versions of the twelve stones mounted on the high priest's vest at the tabernacle, one for each Israelite tribe. "These are the tribal stones, aren't they, Lapp?"

"Yes," said Lapp. "I collected them over the years, not really knowing why—until now."

"Until now?" said Deborah.

"I finally realized they were meant for *you*, because you're a *precious jewel* for me—and for our people."

Deborah slid the bracelet onto her wrist, thinking, *Surely Lapp is God's choice for me!*

To conclude the ceremony—and make it official—Lapp opened a skin of wine and poured some into the wooden goblet. He offered it to Deborah. She looked at Papa, who nodded his approval. The cave was silent except for the voice of a tiny bird singing as it wove its nest in a nearby field. Deborah lifted the goblet to her lips and sipped. Then she shared it with Lapp. They were now engaged.

Deborah and Lapp were married a year later, without the sound of the shofar, and without a noisy celebration; they didn't want to attract the attention of Sisera's troops, who sometimes patrolled the hills.

Years Later . . .

9

THE JUDGE

Lapp and Deborah arose while it was still dark. They dressed quietly, to keep from waking Carmie and the children. Lapp picked up the sack they'd packed the night before. They tiptoed out of the hut, and began their journey to the judging palm.

Deborah was now Judge of Israel, the first woman to hold that title. Every week, she and Lapp walked to a tall palm tree a few miles away. Deborah would sit in the shade of the tree, and listen to arguments and concerns of Israelites from all over Canaan. She settled their disputes, and answered their questions.

Sometimes Deborah decreed punishment for the lawbreakers. Elders from each tribe made sure the penalties were carried out. Lapp always stood near Deborah, to keep her safe.

"Which way are we going today?" whispered Deborah, adjusting her eyes to the moonlight filtering through a thin layer of clouds. They took a different route each time, to keep Sisera's patrols off guard. So far, it had worked.

"Let's go by a pond I found," whispered Lapp, leading Deborah past Carmie's secret vineyard. "If we find game, I'll go back later and try to bag something for dinner."

"We could use some meat," said Deborah. "We haven't had any for a while."

"I know, my love," said Lapp, pulling Deborah close. "I'm sorry. Most of the game has been hunted out."

They walked through the olive grove Carmie had planted years ago. It was fragrant with spring blossoms. Carmie hadn't married, but had stayed with Lapp and Deborah so he could help with their three children—especially on days when the couple traveled to the judging palm.

Deborah followed Lapp through a damp meadow and up a rocky slope, carefully avoiding animal burrows that could break an ankle. After an hour, dawn was breaking and Deborah found herself in an unfamiliar place.

"The pond is right down there," whispered Lapp, pointing to a pool of water at the bottom of a slope. Its surface reflected the pinkish sky. "Let's just skirt it, and see what we flush up."

They silently descended the slope. Lapp stopped abruptly, and pointed to a doe and two fawns lapping at the water. "How lovely!" whispered Deborah. The doe jerked her head up, and twitched her big ears.

Suddenly, a low growling noise sent the deer dashing up the slope past Lapp and Deborah. To their horror, a large hyena followed, nostrils flaring, paws tearing the sod in pursuit of a fawn for breakfast. Deborah shrieked. Lapp stepped between her and the beast, and drew his knife.

The hyena stopped a few yards away, his half-sitting gait out-distanced by the bounding deer. He clawed at the ground, and whined in frustration. The night had yielded nothing to quiet his empty stomach.

Suddenly the beast raised its powerful neck and sniffed. Catching the human scent, he turned and edged closer to Lapp and Deborah. Sizing up Lapp's tall figure, he growled and curled his lips in a menacing snarl, revealing long fangs set in jaws powerful enough to snap a horse's hipbone.

Concealed behind Lapp, Deborah could hear the hyena's breathing, and smell his stench. She remembered stories of people and livestock eaten by hyenas. She prayed silently, *Please, Lord, deliver us!*

With his eyes trained on the predator, Lapp whispered to Deborah, "When I tell you, run for the water. It's safe there. I love you."

"Love you, too" whispered Deborah.

"Now!" shouted Lapp. Deborah took off running for the pond. The hyena was startled to see her appear. Lapp charged the confused animal from the opposite side, to draw him away from Deborah. Baiting the powerful jaws with his wooden staff, Lapp plunged his knife into the hyena's rib cage. The animal howled in pain, and snapped the staff in two. Lapp sank his knife into the muscular neck. The hyena screamed, then staggered to a sitting position. Finally, he fell over and lay gurgling on the ground.

Deborah stood in the pond, terrified. She closed her eyes and prayed. Then it was quiet. When she opened her eyes, Lapp was limping unsteadily toward her, spattered with dark blood. "Oh, thank God!" she exclaimed. "Are you alright?"

"I think so," replied Lapp, checking the bloodstains to make sure none of them were his. Deborah sloshed out of the pond and rushed to Lapp. He held her tightly, thanking God for delivering them. He stopped in mid-sentence. "Wait. I hear something." They listened.

"Horsemen," said Lapp. The hoofbeats drew closer. "They probably heard the hyena." Lapp glanced around for cover. "Quick, the reeds!" He pulled Deborah toward a stand of tall reeds in the water as Sisera's two-man patrol reached the top of the slope. The warriors scanned the landscape.

"There—in the pond," said the taller rider, a scar-faced marauder. He'd caught a glimpse of Deborah ducking behind the reeds. As the soldiers spurred their mounts toward the pond, Lapp realized he was facing a more dangerous foe than the one he'd just killed. Sisera's troops were known for robbing—and sometimes kidnapping—helpless travelers.

The horsemen arrived at the pond. The taller one shouted, "We know you're there! Present yourself in the name of the king!"

Lapp handed Deborah the travel bag, whispering, "Stay down." He stood, and sloshed toward the soldiers, leaving Deborah crouching behind the reeds. She shivered in the cold water, and prayed for help.

"Good morning, sirs!" said Lapp. "What brings you here so early?" The riders noticed the fresh blood on Lapp.

"Where's the beast?" scowled the shorter, fleshier scout. "Has it escaped?"

"No, sir. It lies there," said Lapp, pointing in the direction of the kill. "A fine big hyena, sir. I have no need of him—help yourselves!" The soldier turned his mount and trotted away to inspect the carcass.

"King Jabin *favors* hyena," sneered the tall soldier. "It will make a fine banquet for him." Glancing toward the reeds, he added, "His majesty also favors fine *women* to *serve* it!"

"Sir, what do you mean?" asked Lapp. A surge of fear passed through him. "I am alone here, sir, just ch-checking my traps, I—"

"There!" roared the soldier, pointing to the reeds. "Bring her here, Israelite, or I'll lop off your head!" He drew his sword and began swiping at Lapp, who retreated into the pond where he knew the horse would have poor footing.

The soldier pursued Lapp further and deeper into the water. Lapp dodged the blade again and again. Finally Lapp saw his chance. Knife in hand, he dove under the horse's belly, and slashed the cinch straps, sending the saddle and rider splashing into the pond.

Clad in heavy armor, the attacker sank like a stone. He struggled mightily to gain footing on the slimy bottom, but couldn't. The frightened stallion struggled to the shore and galloped out of sight, leaving his rider cursing and flailing helplessly in the pond.

Alerted by the commotion, the stout soldier returned and charged in after Lapp. As he drew his sword, his horse suddenly reared, frantically pawing the air, as a fat water snake swam toward them. The rider lashed his whip across the horse's head, accidentally striking his own sword, sending it splashing into the pond. He cursed his horse, dismounted, and began searching for his sword.

"Looking for something?" It was Lapp, wielding the sword he'd taken from the fallen attacker. The soldier drew a dagger from his belt. Lapp struck it, knocking it into the water.

"You miserable Israelite," growled the soldier.

"Now hand over that whip," ordered Lapp. "And *not in the water*—or you'll be floating face down!"

"But my—"

"The whip!" roared Lapp, raising the sword. The whip plopped onto the muddy bank. Lapp retrieved it, and called to Deborah, who was watching from the reeds. She emerged soaked and shivering. She hurried toward Lapp.

The soldier was stunned by Deborah's beauty, but chose to insult her. "I see we've been fighting over an Israelite *tramp*," he said. Lapp drew back the whip and landed a stinging blow across the man's face. The soldier staggered backward and landed in the mud with a heavy thud. Blood spurted from his nose.

Lapp grabbed the stallion's reins, hoisted himself to the saddle, then leaned over and pulled Deborah up. She settled into the saddle behind her protector. *Thank you, Lord, for delivering us,* she prayed.

Lapp noticed lingering signs of struggle in the pond. He shouted to the other soldier still writhing on the ground, "I think your friend could use some help!"

The stallion made up for lost time. As Lapp and Deborah neared the judging palm, they dismounted. Lapp removed the horse's saddle and bridle, and gave him a sharp slap on the rump, sending the animal to freedom.

10

FAMILY

"Uncle Carmie! Mama and Papa are back!" cried Sarah. The three children ran to their parents while Carmie watched from the doorway, propped on the crutch Lapp had made him many years before.

Lapp lifted little Marni to his shoulders, where she liked to ride. Nathan felt his father's hunting sack for signs of fresh game. It was empty.

"Sorry, son," said Lapp. "We saw a hyena, but you know we don't eat that kind of meat."

Sarah, the oldest, was almost as tall as Deborah. "Mama!" she cried. "Wait 'til you see my surprise!"

"What a reception!" exclaimed Lapp. "You'd think we'd been gone a week instead of a morning!"

"We're always happy to see you back," said Carmie. "It's so dangerous these days." He noticed the faint blood stains on Lapp's tunic, and the absence of his wooden staff, but didn't ask about them in front of the children.

"God always protects us," said Deborah. The family entered the small hut Lapp had built for the summer months. Sarah poured two cups of cold spring water.

"Thank you, daughter," said Lapp, setting Marni on her feet. He drank the whole cup without stopping. Sarah refilled it. Lapp settled onto a stool next to Deborah.

"How was the judging today?" asked Carmie.

"The usual," answered Deborah. "Housewives arguing over firewood. Men fighting about grazing land. People asking why God has deserted us."

"Some men were arguing over a milking goat," said Lapp.

"Yes," said Deborah. "Three men. One of them was carrying the goat. The first man said the goat had been stolen from him. The second man—the one carrying the goat—said he'd bought it from the third man, in exchange for a pair of gold earrings. The third man denied stealing the goat."

Nathan drew closer, always interested in a crime story. "What did you do, Mama?"

"I asked the man with the goat what the earrings looked like. He said they were shaped like lilies. Papa searched the third man's bag. No earrings. Then he searched the man's headpiece. Guess what fell out?"

"Earrings shaped like lilies!" shouted Nathan. "He was the thief!"

"That's right, son," said Lapp.

"Did you punish him, Mama?" asked Sarah.

"I made him give back the earrings. Papa gave the goat back to the rightful owner."

"And Mama ordered the thief to make a guilt offering at the tabernacle," said Lapp. "God hates lying and stealing."

"Now, we want to hear about what's been happening *here* this morning," said Deborah. "Sarah, what did you say about a surprise?"

"Wait 'til you see!" exclaimed Sarah. She rushed to a shelf and returned with a plate of little cakes.

"Honey cakes!" exclaimed Deborah.

"I made them myself," said Sarah. "One for each of us."

"Where did you get the honey?" asked Lapp.

"Nathan followed the bees," said Sarah. "The hive was in a rock cliff."

"I had to climb way up high!" shouted Nathan. Deborah and Lapp looked at Sarah with raised eyebrows.

"I went with him," Sarah assured them. "And we rubbed oil on him so the bees wouldn't sting."

"Look! No stings!" said Nathan, holding out his arms.

"He was so brave, Papa." said Sarah.

"And *I* squeezed the honey out of the comb, Mama!" boasted Marni, climbing into Deborah's lap.

"She sure did!" said Sarah. "She squeezed out every last drop."

"I'm so proud of all of you!" exclaimed Deborah. Her stomach was growling at the sight of the honey cakes. She and Lapp had skipped breakfast so the children would have enough to eat. She knew the honey cakes had used up their last bit of flour.

"Go ahead and have one, everybody," said Carmie. "This is lunch. Zev and Miriam are bringing our supper tonight!"

"Let's pray first," said Lapp. They bowed their heads. "Thank you, God, for our safe journey this morning," said Lapp. "Thank you for giving Deborah wisdom to judge. I pray this food will keep us strong—to serve you. Amen." They dove into the honey cakes like a family of hungry bears.

11

THE WAY BACK

As the sun sank behind the hills, Zev and Miriam arrived with their two boys, Lubin and Jake, and with Deborah's mother, who was very old. Precious Papa had died trying to save a barley field set on fire by Sisera's troops. That happened before Marni was born.

Supper was the best they'd eaten in weeks. Zev had bagged a wild ram, and Miriam had roasted it all day. The succulent meat was served with gravy, goat cheese, and greens from the meadow. Dessert was wild berries and honeyed cream.

After everyone had stuffed themselves, the children ran to play in the olive grove. The cousins never strayed far. They'd heard about children being kidnapped by Sisera's troops. They knew about an aunt named Ariel who was kidnapped years ago, and never seen again.

"We still pray for Aunt Ariel," said Sarah, her legs dangling from a sturdy branch.

"We do too," said Lubin.

"If I ever see her, I'll recognize her," said Nathan. "She'll look just like Aunt Alissa!"

Meanwhile, the grown-ups sat in front of the hut watching the sunset. They sipped hot tea made from sorrel leaves. The wine had run out months ago.

"How's Alissa today?" asked Deborah. Alissa had just given birth to a baby girl, the second child in her family.

"Better," said Miriam. "She's stronger, but her milk hasn't started yet."

"That's because there isn't enough food for her," said Zev.

"Things have never been *this* bad," said Carmie. "What are we going to do, Deborah?"

"Our people need to turn from their evil ways," said Deborah. "We need to cry out to God to save us. That's what I tell the people at the judging palm."

"People are running wild these days!" fumed Mama. "Instead of taking care of their families, they stay up in the hills getting drunk with the Baal worshippers." Her frail body trembled with emotion. "Imagine! Worshipping a piece of wood!"

"They worship Baal's girlfriend too," said Lapp. "They call her Asherah. She's a tall wooden pole with a carving of a naked woman on top."

"How shameful!" cried Miriam, drawing her shawl tightly around her. "No *wonder* God has turned his back on us!"

"That's what happens when people start inventing gods that let them do whatever they want," said Deborah. "The Asherah worshippers have decided it's alright for men to pretend other men are their wives!" An uncomfortable silence followed.

"Let's talk about something else," said Zev.

"Just one more thing," said Deborah. "We have hope. *Many* people are turning back to God. We've seen them praying together at the wells."

As the sky darkened, revealing a blanket of stars, the children returned from the grove and gathered around the small fire Lapp had built near the hut. They snuggled close to their parents to keep warm against the evening chill. Everyone stared into the flames, mesmerized by the endless patterns of yellow, orange and blue. The wood popped occasionally, sending sparks fluttering skyward.

Zev broke the silence. "Wonderful firewood, Lapp. There isn't much around anymore. Where'd you get it?"

"Well," said Lapp, continuing to stare into the fire, "there's an Asherah pole up on the hill that's a lot shorter tonight!"

12

MESSAGES

One night, Deborah arose without disturbing Lapp. She tiptoed past the sleeping children and Carmie, who was snoring softly. She found her special robe, and slipped outside, quietly closing the door.

Deborah shivered and pulled the heavy robe snugly around her slender body. The robe was given to her by the elders of Israel. It was called an *addereth*. Addereths were only worn by judges. Deborah wore it at the judging palm and when she was doing kingdom business. She also wore it whenever she prayed for Israel.

A brilliant moon hung in the sky. Deborah could see the crest of Mount Tabor far to the north. She stood there for awhile, listening to the night sounds. Then she dropped to her knees next to a wooden bench. She leaned on the bench and took off her bracelet. One by one, she touched the twelve jewels, and prayed for each of Israel's tribes.

Much later, when the moon was pale yellow and sinking behind the western hills, Deborah lifted her face skyward and said, "It will be as you say, Lord."

The next morning, Deborah served her family some leftovers from supper. The children drank the milk Sarah had squeezed from the scrawny she-goat they still kept. Many families had already eaten their milking goats.

When breakfast was over, Deborah gave the children baskets and sent them to a nearby field to pick wild peas. "I think I'll go with them," said Carmie. "It's a beautiful day." The children scampered into the morning sun, with Carmie hobbling after them.

Lapp and Deborah returned to the table to finish their tea. They exchanged warm smiles. Their love had grown stronger over the years. Lapp always knew when Deborah was dealing with something weighty. She would sit quietly, as she did now. He reached for her hand. "What is it, my love?" he asked.

After a moment, Deborah looked steadily at her husband and said, "Israel is to defeat the king's army." Their eyes locked for a moment, then Lapp resumed staring into his tea, trying to absorb the news. He thought about General Sisera's nine hundred iron chariots and his thousands of warriors equipped with swords and armor.

"We haven't any weapons," said Lapp.

"Sisera will be defeated," said Deborah.

"How?"

"God will go before us, and give us the victory."

"How?" persisted Lapp.

"I don't know exactly, but He will."

"Who'll lead us?"

"Barak, son of Abinoam," said Deborah. "He lives at Kedesh."

"Kedesh? That's over a hundred miles from here!"

"I know, but Barak is God's choice. I'm sure of it. I'm sending Zev up there to bring him back. Zev knows every inch of that land from hunting on it."

Deborah knew what Lapp was thinking. "I know you'd like to go with him, Lapp, but we need you here to protect our families. Miriam, Mama, and the children will stay with us while Zev is gone."

Lapp agreed with Deborah's plan, but he was still disappointed to miss the adventure. Seeing his frustration, Deborah said, "If it's adventure you're after, you'll get plenty when we attack King Jabin's army!"

Lapp sensed the powerful Spirit resting on his wife. "So be it," he said.

Two weeks later, Zev arrived back at the hut with Barak. When Deborah heard them talking, she alerted Lapp and quickly slipped into her addereth. They stepped outside and greeted Zev and the visitor. Barak bowed to Deborah, and presented Lapp with a sack of wild game he and Zev had bagged on their trip from Kedesh.

Barak was an older man with graying hair. He held his muscular body tall and straight. A sturdy bow was slung across his back, and a sharp hunting knife flashed on his belt. Deborah thought he looked like an older version of Zev.

Barak bowed to Deborah. "It's an honor to meet you, ma'am. You lead our people with great wisdom."

"Thank you, sir," said Deborah. "It is by God's grace that I lead. And you, sir, are known throughout Israel as a mighty leader of men."

"I serve only through His strength," said Barak.

By this time, Miriam and the children had emerged from the hut, and overpowered Zev with hugs. Deborah introduced them to Barak while Carmie watched from the shade of the doorway. Nathan stared wide-eyed at Barak's powerful bow. "Did you make that bow yourself?" he asked.

"No, I didn't, young man," said Barak with a smile. "There is a man in our tribe who makes these."

"Do you think he could make *me* one?"

"Nathan!" scolded Lapp. "Pleased don't bother Mr. Barak." Miriam and Zev quickly ushered the children into the hut to help prepare the game for supper.

Deborah, Lapp, and Barak moved to the shade of Carmie's olive grove and sat on benches. They talked about the hard life their people were suffering at the hands of the king. People were starving. Desperation was setting in.

Then Deborah looked squarely at Barak and said, "The God of Israel is calling you to serve our people in a new way."

"In a *new* way?" repeated Barak.

"Yes. God is calling you to raise an army of ten thousand Israelite men. You are to lead them to Mount Tabor. God will lure Sisera's troops to the Kishon River below, where He will deliver them to you."

Barak was silent for a moment. Then another. Deborah and Lapp waited quietly for his response. Barak had never led an army. He knew Israel hadn't fought a war in eighty years. He thought about Sisera's nine hundred chariots and thousands of warriors. There wasn't a sword or a shield in all of Israel. They would be outnumbered ten to one.

But Barak also knew that God's favor was with Deborah. Finally, he answered. "I'll go," he said, "but only if you go with me."

"Very well," said Deborah. "I'll go with you."

"When?"

"We'll leave in the morning. We'll recruit fighters as we travel. Do you have some trusted men who can help?"

"Yes, especially from my tribe."

"Good. God will be with us."

That evening, after Zev and Miriam had gone home with their family for the night, Deborah and Lapp gathered their children. Deborah's mother, Carmie, and Barak listened nearby.

Lapp spoke first. "Mama and I will be leaving very early in the morning."

"But tomorrow isn't judging day!" said Sarah.

"That's right, Sarah," said Lapp, "but we need to go on a special trip for our people. We'll be going up to Mount Tabor."

"Can *we* go?" asked Nathan.

"I'm sorry, son, but this is a special trip just for grown-ups. Uncle Zev and Mr. Barak will be going with us."

"But who'll stay with *us*?" asked Sarah.

"Uncle Carmie and Uncle Eli," said Deborah. "Aunt Miriam, Grandma, Jake, and Rubin will stay here too."

Sarah was frightened at the thought of her parents being gone so long. "When will you be back?" she asked.

"We don't know exactly," explained Lapp. "Some other people are making the trip too."

"I don't like this one bit," declared Sarah, crossing her arms. "This is *scaring* me!" Marni climbed onto Deborah's lap and began sucking her thumb.

"Now listen everybody," said Deborah. She pulled all three children into her arms. "If Papa and I aren't scared, you shouldn't be scared either. God wants us to make this trip, so He'll protect *all* of us. I *promise!*"

13

THE BATTLE

Deborah hadn't been to Mount Tabor since she was a girl. Sometimes Mama and Papa had taken the family there for a day or two of hunting and fishing. Deborah had always felt closer to God there among the things He'd made; the majestic trees, the graceful deer, the songbirds, the delicate orchids.

As a girl, Deborah had lain on the soft moss at night and gazed at the endless stars, marveling at God's vast universe. She wondered what it would be like to die and be taken to some glorious place out there—a place where she would see angels, her ancestors, and God.

Now Deborah, Lapp, Zev, and Barak traveled at night—in the hills—to avoid Sisera's patrols. They hid during the day. They quietly collected an army of Israelites from the hill country. Barak sent messages to all twelve tribes, asking them to send fighters.

As they neared the mountain, Deborah stopped abruptly, startled by its appearance. The slopes were marred by ugly stretches of bare ground. "What happened up there?" she asked.

"They cut down trees to build Jabin's cities," said Zev.

As they skirted around the Kishon River, Deborah noticed its once crystal water was now brown and murky. "Where is all this mud coming from?" she asked.

"When the slopes are stripped bare, the dirt gets washed down," explained Zev.

"And it smothers the fish," added Lapp.

"Remember the trout I caught here?" said Zev.

"Yes, I remember," answered Lapp. "You'll never let me forget it!"

"Those were good times," said Zev. "The land is suffering under Jabin too."

Deborah's group reached Kedesh and collected more men, food, and tenting supplies. Then they made their way to the north slope of Mount Tabor. A small patrol led by Barak climbed to the summit to stake out a camp. Other units climbed at night.

Deborah, Lapp, and Zev began their ascent at sundown one evening. By the time they reached the summit, morning had dawned and Deborah's gown was caked with mud up to her knees. Her sandals had been shredded by the jagged rocks, leaving her barefoot.

When they arrived at the camp, Barak greeted them. "Praise God for delivering you safely!" he said. "Let me show you to your quarters."

"We've brought our own tents," said Zev.

Noticing the crowded camp, Deborah said, "I'm sure our tents can be put to good use." Many of the fighters had little more than their ragged clothing and homemade weapons.

Deborah and Lapp found their tent simple but comfortable. Once inside, Deborah lit an oil lamp and changed into some dry clothes. Later that day, Deborah, Lapp, and Zev met with Barak at the command post, Barak's tent. "Do we have ten thousand fighters yet?" asked Deborah.

"We're close," said Barak. "I'm expecting more tomorrow and the next day. We'll reach the number soon."

"Have all the tribes sent men?" asked Lapp.

"Most have, but some haven't," answered Barak.

"Some men put their own business ahead of God's!" fumed Zev. "We'll do the fighting for *them* too!"

"How are the men's spirits?" asked Deborah.

"We're short on food and weapons, but they're ready to fight. They know this is a battle for their families."

As the army neared the ten thousand mark, the rumble of chariots was heard in the valley below. Day by day, the riverbanks filled with hundreds of tents, chariots, horses, pack animals, and the king's fighters.

At night, cooking fires dotted the enemy camp. The clanging of swords could be heard as the warriors practiced for the battle. *God has lured them here, as He promised,* thought Deborah.

On the mountaintop, fear began to grip the Israelites. There was talk of fleeing for home, while there was still time. Deborah, Lapp, and Zev mingled with the troops night and day, praying with them, and assuring them that God would keep His word, and give them victory.

"There are ten of them for every one of us!" cried one man.

"We're weak from hunger, ma'am," complained another. "How can we fight men who are well fed?"

"Because we are weak, God will be strong for us," answered Deborah. "The victory will be His."

One afternoon, Barak and his aides walked through the camp, counting the men. Afterward, he went to Deborah and said, "Ma'am, the mark has been reached."

"Thank you, Barak. And thank you for assembling the army. Please post guards tonight. See that no one leaves."

"Yes ma'am," said Barak.

As she and Lapp entered their tent for the night, Deborah paused and scanned the western sky. Storm clouds gathered in the distance.

The next morning, Deborah awoke to the sound of thunder. Rain pelted the tent. She nudged Lapp awake, and sent him for Barak and Zev. Pulling her addereth around her, she stepped into the wet, foggy dawn.

Lapp, Zev, and Barak soon hurried toward her as the rain became a downpour, soaking their clothes and dripping from their noses and chins. A clap of thunder shook the mountain. Lightning flashed across the sky, causing the men to cry out in their flimsy tents. Zev lifted the tent flap for Deborah and the others to enter.

"Wait," said Deborah. "It is time."

"Time?" asked Barak.

"It is time to attack," said Deborah.

"But ma'am, we can't attack in this storm. We'll have no footing, we—"

"Barak," said Deborah, "this is the day the Lord will deliver Sisera to you. God's hand goes before you. Now *go!*"

Thunder cracked, and the heavens spilled forth a torrent of rain, as Barak roused his army. The ground turned to mud. Barak climbed to the top of a boulder near the mountain's summit. Deborah and Lapp joined him. The Israelite fighters gathered around them. The men were quiet and somber as the moment of battle approached.

"Men of Israel!" shouted Barak over the roar of the storm. "Sisera has his horses and chariots! He has his warriors, but *we* fight in the name of the God of Israel! Today the Lord will deliver our enemy into our hands, and the world will know that He is God."

Barak raised his spear. A roar went up from the Israelites. At Barak's signal, they charged down the slope toward Sisera's army. Deborah watched Lapp and Zev join the sea of men that disappeared over the crest of the mountain.

"The Lord go with you," she whispered. She remained on the boulder, her face toward heaven. She lifted her arms and shouted, "God of creation, bless us indeed! Thank you for delivering us from our enemy this day!"

Sheets of water poured down the slope. The earth shook violently, sending men and giant boulders tumbling. Israelites grabbed tree trunks to keep from being swept to a muddy death. They clung to branches as they made their way down. As they neared the bottom, they could hear the whinnying of horses, and the shouts of men.

When the Israelites reached the bottom of the mountain, they beheld a scene of utter chaos. Chariots were sinking in the mud. Soldiers viciously whipped their horses in an effort to free the heavy vehicles. Men and animals screamed as they were swept away in the swollen river.

Pack animals roared in terror as they struggled to flee the rising flood. Men clung desperately to the boulders that had landed in the water, but the ferocious river soon washed over their heads. Water spilled over the riverbanks, flooding the camp. Tents and poles floated downstream. Soldiers sloshed about, dazed and confused.

When Sisera's troops saw the ten thousand Israelites gathered on the slope, they were panic-stricken. Barak's army released a shower of arrows. Thousands of them found their mark. Those who survived tried to escape to higher ground, but the Israelites blocked their way, cutting them down by the thousands.

Sisera and his entire army died that day. Not a single man remained. The nine hundred chariots were gone too, entombed in the mud with their horses. The victorious Israelites took no spoils from the battle—no weapons, no horses, no treasure. They headed home with only their crude weapons—and thankful hearts.

The battle became known as *The Miracle at Mount Tabor*. Word of it spread throughout Canaan and the neighboring lands. When the news reached King Jabin, he fled and was never heard from again.

Baal worship ceased. Asherah poles were pulled down and burned. The people turned from their evil ways and worshipped the one true God again. Canaan was at peace.

14

HOME

A few weeks after the battle, Carmie stood in the old watchtower, smiling down on his new vineyard. He saw the village bustling with life again. Homes were being built by Lapp and his crew of carpenters. Children played in the courtyard. Women planted gardens. Shepherds tended their flocks on the hillsides. Nathan practiced shooting the handsome bow Barak had given him, using a stuffed sheepskin as a target.

Now Lapp and Deborah could travel to the judging palm on a safe road. Deborah was at home one day, teaching Sarah how to make Passover bread. "Just a little more water," said Deborah. Sarah dribbled a few more drops into the flour, and continued to stir. Marni sat on the floor, playing with the new doll Lapp had carved for her, and snacking on raisins.

"Didn't we forget the yeast, Mama?" asked Sarah.

"Passover bread doesn't have yeast," said Deborah. "That's why it's flat. When our people escaped from Egypt, there wasn't time for the bread to rise."

"I love flat bread," said Marni. "I like to dip it in my stew." She pretended to feed her doll a raisin.

Suddenly Nathan bounded through the door. "Mama! Mama!" he yelled. "There's a lady looking for you! I think it's Aunt Ariel!"

"What?" gasped Deborah.

"She looks just like Aunt Alissa!" cried Nathan.

"Are you sure?"

"Positive!"

"Where?" said Deborah, suddenly feeling her heart pounding wildly.

"Come on!" Nathan charged back outside. Deborah and the girls followed him to a neighbor's house where a crowd was gathered outside. In the middle stood a thin woman and a little girl. They were barefoot and in rags.

As Deborah neared the group, the woman was saying, "Yes, I'm the twin of Alissa, daughter of—" She saw Deborah approaching. "Deborah!" she cried.

"Ariel!" Deborah rushed to her sister. They clung to each other for a long time, as if making up for all the hugs they'd missed. Finally, Deborah looked into Arial's face again. "I can't believe it's *really you!*" exclaimed Deborah, though Ariel was the image of Alissa, only thinner.

"I know!" cried Ariel. "I'd given up ever seeing you again." She realized she was now taller than Deborah. Soon Miriam arrived with her children and Mama, whose fragile body trembled as she embraced her lost daughter.

"My precious child!" sobbed Mama. "We never gave up hope for you! If only Papa could see you!"

"Papa?" asked Ariel with alarm. A hush came over the onlookers.

"Yes, my child. He has been gone from us many seasons." Ariel's shoulders drooped at the news. She hugged Mama tenderly.

Deborah joined the hug, and whispered to Ariel, "Papa never stopped grieving for you, Ariel. You were always his *little lamb*."

Just then, Arial noticed a mirror image of herself approaching with a baby in her arms. The woman's eyes brimmed with tears. "Alissa!" Ariel grabbed her little girl by the hand and rushed to her twin. After a long hug, Ariel turned to Alissa's baby. "And who is this beautiful child?"

"She's our daughter," said Alissa. "We named her Ariel!"

Ariel lifted her own daughter so she could see the baby. "See? This is your baby cousin. Her name is Ariel, just like me!" The girl smiled shyly at the baby, and then at Alissa. "And this is your Aunt Alissa," said Ariel, "my twin I've always told you about."

"She looks like you, Mama." said the girl.

"And what's *your* name?" asked Alissa.

The child looked shyly away and began chewing on her grimy fingers. "Go ahead," coaxed Ariel. "Tell her your name."

The child pulled her fingers out of her mouth, smiled bashfully at her aunt and replied, "My name is Alissa—just like you!"

That evening the whole family gathered at Deborah and Lapp's house for the Passover meal. The children played outside, while Deborah and Miriam hustled about in the kitchen. The rest of the grown-ups surrounded Ariel, plying her with questions about her lost years as a slave. Mama rocked baby Ariel, who slept contently in her arms.

"When I was first taken," said Ariel, "I was put to work as a spinner near the king's palace. I spun wool into yarn all day."

"By yourself?" ask Carmie.

"No, there were other slave girls. One was an Israelite, so I had someone to talk to."

"How did they treat you?" asked Zev.

"Badly. There wasn't much to eat, and we slept on the floor. They beat us when we were too sick to work." Alissa pulled her sister close. Seen together, Ariel looked more like an older sister than a twin. Slavery had aged her.

"When I was old enough to marry," continued Arial, "I was *sold* to an officer in Sisera's army. He had other wives besides me. He was cruel to *all* of us." Ariel's lip trembled. "He—he was little Alissa's *father.*" She squeezed back tears.

"It's alright, Ariel," said Alissa, hugging her twin. "You're home now. It's *safe* here, and life will be *good* again."

"How did you escape?" asked Zev.

"The whole army was killed at Mt. Tabor, including my husband," said Ariel. "When the news reached the city, everyone fled. We ran off and hid in the woods."

"How did you get here?" asked Carmie.

"We hid during the day and walked at night. I couldn't trust anyone, even though I knew Deborah was Judge of Israel. Who would believe me? I was afraid of being taken as a slave again."

"What did you eat?" asked Lapp.

"We ate wild plants, the ones I knew weren't poison. We got *so hungry* that I almost stole some food, but I knew it was wrong."

"The Passover's ready!" announced Deborah. Miriam called the children in from the courtyard. They crowded around the wash basin, but let their newfound cousin, Alissa, go first. Miriam lit the oil lamps. The room took on a warm glow.

When everyone was seated, Deborah placed the platter of roast lamb in front of Lapp. Sarah proudly presented her flat bread. Miriam set a bowl of bitter greens and salt water on the table. Marni made a face. "Mama, why do we have to eat these yucky leaves?"

"Because we need to remember how *bitter* it was to be a slave in Egypt," said Deborah.

"But *I* wasn't a slave in Egypt!"

"You're right, Marni, but we'd still be slaves if God hadn't rescued Israel. He also freed Aunt Ariel and Cousin Alissa. Just eat a little—for *them*."

Lapp raised his hands and eyes toward heaven. Everyone bowed their heads. "You are the one true God," said Lapp. "You freed our people from Egypt! You defeated Jabin's army! You delivered our precious Ariel and—" Lapp's voice broke with emotion—"and little Alissa, safely home." Lapp paused to compose himself. "We thank you for this food that you have brought forth from the earth. May it strengthen us to serve you. Amen."

Lapp tore off a piece of bread and gave it to Deborah. Marni reached for the bitter leaves. *Praise God for everything that's good!* thought Deborah.

When the meal was over, and the new arrivals had gone home with Alissa's family, Lapp and Deborah said prayers with Sarah, Nathan, and Marni. The children nestled into their beds, and listened to Deborah's bedtime story. She told them how their ancestor, Moses, had led their people out of slavery long ago. "We need to be like Moses," said Deborah, "and believe God for things that seem impossible."

As the children drifted off to sleep, Lapp and Deborah tiptoed outside and settled onto a bench by Deborah's new garden. A summer moon rose in the east. A blanket of stars twinkled overhead. Deborah snuggled close to Lapp and gazed up at the heavens.

Lapp thought Deborah was more beautiful than ever, despite the years of hardship. He noticed her bracelet, and remembered their engagement night long ago.

"Were you ever tempted to sell your bracelet to buy food?" he asked.

"Yes, there were *many* times," said Deborah. "There were days when we had *nothing* left to eat, but I always trusted God for just *one more meal*. He always provided it, so I never had to sell my bracelet!"

"That's like the history of Israel," said Lapp. "There were times when it looked like our people were doomed to disappear, but God always raised up someone like you to lead us back to him. He always rescued enough of us to keep Israel alive."

"Yes," said Deborah, "and I *pray* He doesn't have to do it again for a *very long time!*"

Deborah's prayer was answered. The nation of Israel lived in peace for many years after that. To this day, Deborah is remembered as the mother and judge in Israel who led her people with truth, wisdom, and courage.

If my people, who are called by my name,
will humble themselves and pray and seek my face
and turn from their wicked ways,
then I will hear from heaven
and will forgive their sins
and will heal their land.

2 Chronicles 7:14

ACKNOWLEDGEMENTS

Jane Clark, Cindy Gatten, Mary Gunderson, Joan Hamilton, and Beth Williams for their invaluable proofreading and feedback. John Gunderson for his patience. God for his goodness

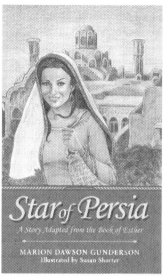

Paperback and e-book copies of
Jewel of Canaan and *Star of Persia* by
Marion Dawson Gunderson are available at:
www.amazon.com
www.barnesandnoble.com
www.bookstore.westbowpress.com

To learn more about the The Brave Beauty Series, visit:
www.BraveBeautyBooks.com
Contact the author at: BraveBeautyBooks@aol.com